Postman Pat® and the Job Swap Day

SIMON AND SCHUSTER

It was a wet day in Greendale. Drops of rain plip-plopped through the
school roof into the mugs and buckets which Jeff Pringle had put out.

"We must get that roof fixed," groaned Jeff. "I'm running out of cups!"

"We don't have enough money yet," sighed Reverend Timms, pointing
to the repair fund chart. "What we need is a miracle!"

Just then, Pat arrived. "Hello everyone! I've got a fundraising idea – a sponsored job swap! Look, I've written people's jobs down on bits of paper. All you have to do is pick one out of my hat, and then everyone in the village will pay you to do that job for the day!"

They all agreed it was a brilliant idea.

The vicar was the first to pick.

"Ah! I've got your job, Alf. I'm going to be a farmer!"

"And I'm going to be a teacher!" chuckled Alf. "I'll teach those kids a thing or two, eh, Jeff?"

Next was Ted. "By 'eck, looks like I'm working in the cafe. That should be a doddle!"

"And we've got Ted's job for the day," smiled Nisha. "What will we be doing, Ted?" Sara asked.

"Decorating Dr Gilbertson's living room!" grinned Ted.

"That's sorted then. Good luck, everybody!" said Pat. "I'd better get on with my rounds. I'll pop in and see you all later."

Reverend Timms set off to tend his flock. "Ah, lovely fresh air. I could get used to this," he thought dreamily, forgetting to close the gate behind him . . .

Back in the classroom, Alf was giving a maths lesson.

"Now, let's see. If you have five sheep, and er . . . you take three away . . . how many are left?"

The children looked bored.

"Two, sir!" said Charlie Pringle. "That's easy!"

"This teaching lark isn't easy!" muttered Alf.

Pat was just delivering the post to the vicarage, when he heard a bleating noise coming from the church.

"I wonder what's going on, Jess. It's a bit early for choir practice! Let's take a look."

A sheep was munching away at the church flowers!

"Heh heh!" chortled Pat. "We'd better tell the vicar one of his flock has strayed!"

"Miaow!" agreed Jess . . .

. . . and chased the poor sheep up the aisle, around the church, out through the door . . .

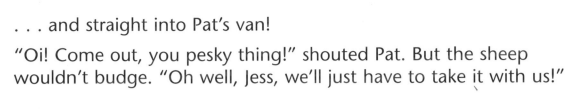

. . . and straight into Pat's van!

"Oi! Come out, you pesky thing!" shouted Pat. But the sheep wouldn't budge. "Oh well, Jess, we'll just have to take it with us!"

Pat made his way to the cafe, where Ted was in full swing.

"Customers need to be served more quickly," he announced. "I've put a motor on the cake stand, see? It turns all by itself now."

The cake stand started to speed up, faster and faster, sending cakes flying everywhere. Dr Gilbertson got splattered with cream and a ring doughnut landed on PC Selby's nose!

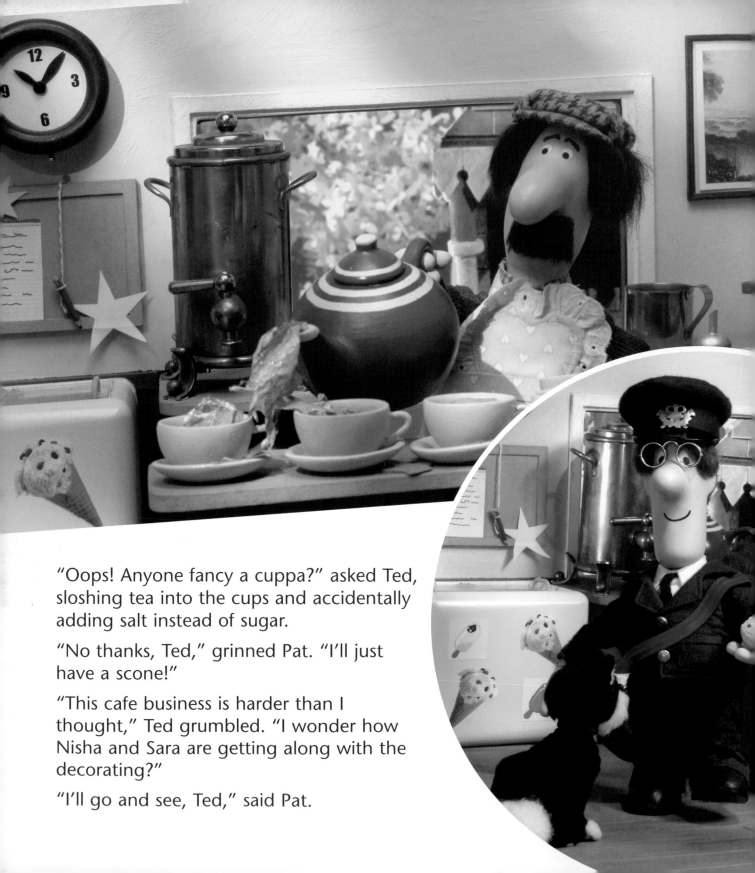

"Oops! Anyone fancy a cuppa?" asked Ted, sloshing tea into the cups and accidentally adding salt instead of sugar.

"No thanks, Ted," grinned Pat. "I'll just have a scone!"

"This cafe business is harder than I thought," Ted grumbled. "I wonder how Nisha and Sara are getting along with the decorating?"

"I'll go and see, Ted," said Pat.

When Pat got back to his van, the sheep was munching its way through the post.

"Oi! Leave those letters alone!" shouted Pat. He gave the sheep his scone to chew instead.

At Dr Gilbertson's house, Nisha and Sara were in a bit of a pickle. There was wallpaper everywhere, even over the doorway, and Sara had dropped a pot of paste on Nisha's head!

Pat and Jess tore right through the wallpaper. Pat glanced around.
"Hum, I see you've been busy!"

"We got a bit carried away," said Nisha.

"We'll stick to the cafe from now on!" Sara laughed.

Meanwhile, the children were having an unusual games lesson.

"Now," Alf explained, "you are all sheep, and when I blow my whistle, I want you to follow my instructions."

The children got in a terrible muddle and it took Alf some time to round them up!

"By gum, I don't have this much trouble with my sheep!" he tutted.

Reverend Timms was having a spot of bother with his sheep too. Pat and Jess were collecting the mail from the country post box when they bumped into him.

"Don't worry, Reverend, we'll give you a hand," offered Pat.

Pat managed to get his stray sheep out of his van, and Jess the sheep-dog rounded the rest of the flock back into their field.

"Come on, Reverend," smiled Pat. "I'll give you a lift to school, and we'll collect the sponsor money on the way."

Back at the school hall, everyone was looking worn out from their day's work.

"I'd like to thank everyone for taking part in the sponsored job swap," said Pat. "I think you'll all agree that it's proved quite a challenge!"

They certainly did agree!

"Right," said Jeff, "we've counted up the money you've raised, and we've reached our target. Now we can get the roof fixed!"

"Well done, everyone," said Pat. "You're all very clever. I couldn't do any of your jobs, and thanks to you, it won't rain inside school any more!"

"Hurray!" they all cheered.

SIMON AND SCHUSTER
First published in 2005 in Great Britain by Simon & Schuster UK Ltd
Africa House, 64-78 Kingsway
London WC2B 6AN

Postman Pat® © 2005 Woodland Animations, a division of Entertainment Rights PLC
Licensed by Entertainment Rights PLC
Original writer John Cunliffe
From the original television design by Ivor Wood
Royal Mail and Post Office imagery is used by kind permission of Royal Mail Group plc
All rights reserved

Text by Alison Ritchie © 2005 Simon & Schuster UK Ltd

A CIP catalogue record for this book is available from the British Library upon request

ISBN 0 689 87559 2

Printed in China

1 3 5 7 9 10 8 6 4 2